To the children of the world, who I hope will be inspired to do
great things in a small way.

AG

Inspired by Parkside Community School and the Protea Pod: Joe, Claire,
Shannon, and Karen. This one is for you.

BH

To Charlie, Isa, Simón, and Santi, who inspired me to be the best person
I could be, and to leave a better world for them.

AL

First edition 2023

Library of Congress Catalog Card Number 2022908132
ISBN 978-1-5362-1744-5

23 24 25 26 27 28 CCP 10 9 8 7 6 5 4 3 2 1

Printed in Shenzhen, Guangdong, China

This book was typeset in Bauer Grotesk.
The illustrations were done in watercolor pencil and gouache.

Candlewick Press
99 Dover Street
Somerville, Massachusetts 02144

www.candlewick.com

You, Me, We

A Celebration of Peace and Community

Arun Gandhi and Bethany Hegedus

illustrated by Andrés Landazábal

CANDLEWICK PRESS

Where do we find peace?

Is peace in you?
Is peace in me?

Peace is in the way we walk,
the way we sit,

the way we stand,
the way we form a circle.

Peace is in the way we play—
rolling up our sleeves,

alfalfa

turnips

carrots

digging in the dirt,
watching a caterpillar wiggle!

Peace is in speaking up.

"Ouch! That hurts."

"It's my turn. I'm next."

"Can you please help me with my zipper?"

Peace is in sitting still.

Crisscross applesauce.

Eyes closed.

Deep breath.

Listening to the silence.

Alone
or together.

And sometimes
alone together.

Peace is in a gentle shake.
Peace isn't order for order's sake.

Peace is in returning things to their proper place.
Peace isn't something that can break.

Peace is in learning—

adding,

subtracting,

counting,

coloring.

Peace is in
you having your part

and me having mine.

Peace is in *all* of our voices being heard.

Peace isn't always easy to find.
There can be misunderstandings,
angry words,
hurt feelings.

But if we look at each other,
ready to discover,

peace is always there.

Peace is in small moments,

big moments,

all moments.

Peace is you.

Peace is me.

Peace is the great big WE . . .

of community.

Authors' Note

Is peace in you? Is peace in me? And what about when we are a great big we?

A community is made up of individuals. There are many different kinds of communities, including families, schools, and neighborhoods. A family may include parents, grandparents, and siblings. A school includes students, teachers, and families. A neighborhood contains streets with houses and apartment buildings, various places of worship, local businesses, and parks to play and enjoy nature in. In all of these communities, we learn independence as well as how to come together.

You, Me, We: A Celebration of Peace and Community was inspired by the words of Mahatma Gandhi and his friendship with and influence on the work of Maria Montessori, an educator and the creator of the Montessori Method, which continues to thrive in school communities all across the world. Addressing a group of Montessori teachers in training in London in 1931, Gandhi said, "If we are to teach real peace in this world . . . we shall have to begin with children."

According to the Montessori Method, allowing children to follow their curious nature guides them toward peace. Through joyful questioning, exploring our inner and outer worlds, examining conflict as it occurs, and coming together as individuals in community, we can build a peaceful world.

What questions do you have about peace? About community? Discuss them with your family, in your schools, in your communities. All of us together—you, me, and we—can build a lasting peace.